Enid B

The Very Peculiar Cow

...and other stories

BB Bounty
BOOKS

Published in 2015 by Bounty Books,
a division of Octopus Publishing Group Ltd,
Carmelite House
50 Victoria Embankment,
London EC4Y 0DZ
www.octopusbooks.co.uk

An Hachette UK Company
www.hachette.co.uk
Enid Blyton ® Text copyright © 2011 Chorion Rights Ltd.
Illustrations copyright © 2015 Award Publications Ltd.
Layout copyright © 2015 Octopus Publishing Group Ltd.

Illustrated by Sara Silcock.

ISBN: 978-0-75372-964-9

A CIP catalogue record for this book is available from the
British Library.

Printed and bound by CPI Group (UK) Ltd, Croydon, CR0 4YY

CONTENTS

CONTENTS

The Very
Peculiar Cow

When Granny came to tea she always brought a parcel with her for Jane and William to undo. Inside there was a present.

One day she brought a parcel that had a most peculiar shape.

"Let me feel it," begged Jane. "Just to see if I can guess what's inside, Granny."

She felt it. "It's got legs," she said. "I'm sure it's a toy animal. Is it, Granny?"

"Not exactly," said Granny.

Then William felt all over the parcel, and he thought it was an animal, too.

They undid it – and whatever do you suppose it was? It was a white china cow, and in its back was a little china lid that fitted there like a teapot lid!

"Why does this china cow have a lid?"

said Jane, in wonder. "I've never seen a cow with a lid in its back before. What do you keep inside it, then? Money?"

"Oh no," said Granny. "I'll show you. I had this cow when I was a little girl, and I loved it. I found it yesterday when I was turning out old trunks – so I brought it along for you. Now watch."

She went to the tea-table and set the china cow down beside the cups. She took the lid off its back and showed the children the cow's hollow body inside. Then she filled the cow with milk!

"Now," she said, "we all know that milk comes from the cow – and it does from this one, too!" Granny tipped up the cow and from its open mouth the milk poured steadily out into Jane's mug!

She gave a squeal of delight. "Oh, Granny! It's a cow jug! It really pours milk. Doesn't it look funny coming out of its mouth! Can we really keep it and use it every day?"

"Yes," said Granny. "I'll give it to you both. You can each take turns at pouring out the milk."

William and Jane loved the white china cow. It had a nice face, two china horns, and very nice black eyes. They both loved pouring their milk from it, and when the cow was not being used at tea-time or breakfast-time Mummy stood it safely up on the mantelpiece.

"We want to see it, not have it put away in the cupboard with the teapot," said Jane. "And I'm sure the cow would rather be where it can see everyone, too. Perhaps it will make friends with the toys at night."

"I shall put one of my little toy horses up on the mantelpiece with it," said William. "You put your little farmhouse dog, too, Jane. And we'll put the two sheep out of the Noah's Ark. It won't feel lonely then."

So they put the little wooden horse on the mantelpiece with the cow, and they put the dog from Jane's toy farm, and the two Noah's Ark sheep there too.

But none of them would make friends with the cow! At night they turned their backs, and just talked to one another. The cow gave a little friendly moo, but they took no notice.

"Hey, you up there!" called the teddy-bear that night. "Bring the cow down for a game."

"No," said the horse. "It's a silly cow. It isn't a toy, and it isn't an ornament."

"And it's really rather disgusting," said the farm-dog, who thought he knew all about cows because he lived on a toy farm. "It pours milk out of its mouth, of all things."

"As if it was being sick," said the two sheep, together. "*We've* never seen a cow behave like that before, and we've met plenty."

"I can't help pouring milk out of my mouth," said the china cow. "Don't be unkind."

"He says we're unkind now," said the dog, and he ran at the china cow and began to bark. "Pooh! Woof, woof! Call

yourself a cow. You're nothing but a milk jug made like a cow!"

"I'm a cow," said the china cow. "Jane and William said so. And they called me Clover."

"Fancy calling a milk jug Clover!" said the horse, and he neighed and laughed. "Clover, Clover, push him over!" He ran at the cow as if he meant to knock her off the mantelpiece. The cow backed away in alarm.

"Don't do that," she said. "I'm only

10

made of china. I should break. And don't call me 'he'. I'm a 'she'. Cows are always shes."

"You're not a cow. You're a jug," said the dog. "We'll call you 'it'. Look, Teddy, 'it' is afraid of falling off the mantelpiece!"

The poor china cow didn't have a very good time at night. The teddy-bear sometimes climbed up and got on her back and tried to gallop her off the mantelpiece. The toy clown climbed up one night and filled her with tiny beads, and then poured them out of her mouth all over the mantelpiece.

Everyone squealed with laughter, and there was a dreadful mess of beads everywhere. The cow didn't like it at all. She backed away behind the clock, and hid there.

When the toys found that they could pour all kinds of things out of the cow's mouth they all took it in turns to put something silly inside her, and then pour it out by tipping her up suddenly.

They filled her with pins and poured those out! They filled her with sugar

from the basin and poured that all over the place.

"What a shocking waste!" said the poor cow. She didn't like the sweet taste in her mouth, either. She really did have a bad time, because the toys weren't a bit friendly to her.

And then one night something horrid happened.

The teddy-bear was up on the mantelpiece, just about to put some glue into the cow, for a joke, when he heard a scream from down below on the

hearthrug. He dropped the glue and ran to peep over the edge of the mantelpiece.

There was a fire in the fireplace, with a log of wood burning there. The toys had come to sit on the hearthrug to warm themselves – and some sparks had leapt out and fallen on the hearthrug – and in a second there was a smell of burning, and a little flame sprang up.

"Fire! Fire!" cried the teddy-bear in fright. "Get some water, quick!"

But there was no water to get. The bathroom was a long way away, and the nursery door was shut, so it wasn't any good sending someone to turn on a tap in the far-away bathroom!

The little flame ate up a bit of the

13

carpet and began on another bit. It made a bigger flame, and reached out to the edge of the baby doll's dress. She screamed.

The cow heard all the excitement and she went to peep over the mantelpiece too.

"Good gracious!" she said. "In another minute all the rug will be ablaze! Teddy, do what I tell you, quick!"

"What, oh, what?" cried the frightened teddy-bear.

"See that vase of flowers on the end of the mantelpiece?" said the cow. "It's full of water. Tip out the flowers and drag the vase here."

The teddy-bear did as he was told. He tipped out the flowers, and dragged the vase up to the china cow.

"Now tip the vase over carefully, and pour some of the water into the hole in my back," said the cow. "My lid is off, so I'm ready. Quick, Teddy!"

With trembling hands the teddy-bear tipped up the vase, and let the water trickle into the hole in the cow's back. "Enough!" said the cow, and went

carefully to the edge of the mantelpiece.
She looked over. Yes – there were the
flames just below, eating up the rug.

"Tip me up," she ordered the teddy-
bear, and Teddy tipped her from the
back. Out poured the water from the

china cow's mouth, tumbling from the mantelpiece like a waterfall, straight down to the burning rug!

Sizzle, sizzle, sizzle, sizz! Some of the flames went out at once, and black smoke came instead.

"Now fill me again," said the cow, and the teddy-bear obeyed. Then up the cow was tipped once more, and out of her mouth fell the water till she was quite empty.

"Once more, and I think all the flames will be out." said the cow, and for the third time she was filled, tipped up and spouted water down to the rug below. Sizzle-sizzle! The last of the flames went out, and now, except for a nasty smell and drifts of smoke, there was nothing left of the fire on the hearthrug.

"You very clever cow!" shouted up the toy-clown in delight. "How did you think of doing that?"

"It was easy," said the cow. "I'm used to pouring out of my mouth."

"You're a wonder and a marvel!" shouted up the sailor doll. "Can't you come down here and play with us?"

The china cow felt delighted. "But you've always laughed at me and teased me before," she said. "And the horse and dog and sheep up here have been very unkind."

"We're sorry," said the horse, and he hung his head. "Aren't we, sheep and dog?"

"Yes," said the others. "Come on, cow – let's go down and play with the toys."

"I can't climb down like you," said the

17

cow. "I'm made of china, and if I slipped I'd break into bits."

"Well, then, we'll all come up!" shouted the teddy-bear. "It's a big mantelpiece, and if you push back the clock and the vase we could all get on."

What an evening that was! The mantelpiece was so crowded that the woolly bunny got knocked off – but he didn't hurt himself when he fell to the floor because he really was so very, very soft.

They all played silly games, and they made such a fuss of the china cow that she felt quite shy. And when the baby doll found out that it was the cow's birthday the next night she had a wonderful idea.

"We'll all come up here and drink your health out of the toy teacups," she said. "We'll get some lemonade from the dolls'-house larder – and *you*, cow, shall pour it into the cups for us – out of your mouth!"

"Ah – now I know you really like me," said the cow, happily. "I *shall* l ook forward to tomorrow night – and

I'll pour my very best and not spill a single drop!"

I wish I could peep into the playroom and watch what goes on up there on the mantelpiece. I should like to drink the china cow's health in lemonade, too!

The Land
of Nowhere

Daniel and Susie had a pet between them. They loved it very much indeed. It was a pure white rabbit with big, floppy ears and a lovely nose that twitched up and down. They called it Snowball, and every day they gave their rabbit fresh lettuce to eat and cleaned out its hutch.

"He's the loveliest rabbit in the world," Daniel said, and Susie thought so too. The children had no other pets – just Snowball; so they loved the rabbit very much, and played with him as often as they could.

Then one day a dreadful thing happened. They went to Snowball's hutch after breakfast – and the door was wide open. Daniel peeped into the hutch and looked all round. There was no rabbit there!

"Susie!" he cried. "What's happened? Snowball's gone! However could he have opened the door?"

"He couldn't have," said Susie, in astonishment. "I shut it myself yesterday evening and made it fast. I remember doing it."

"Yes, I saw you," said Daniel. "Then how could Snowball have escaped?"

"Somebody let him out," said Susie, nearly crying.

"Oh, it's too bad! Let's look for him."

So they looked for Snowball everywhere. They called him and hunted for him all over the garden. But he was gone. There wasn't a sign of him anywhere at all.

Susie sat down in the grass and cried loudly. Daniel was very worried too. He did so love Snowball, and it was dreadful not to know where he was. Suppose – just suppose – someone had stolen him and meant to have him for dinner! It was too dreadful to think of. Daniel didn't dare to tell Susie what he thought, for he knew she would be very unhappy.

Then a strange thing happened and their adventures began. They heard a

shrill whistling not far off, very high and strange. The children looked at one another.

"Where does that whistling come from?" asked Susie, drying her eyes.

"It sounds as if it came from the greenhouse," said Daniel, puzzled. "But surely it can't, because there's no one there. Let's go and look."

So they went. The door was open, and they went inside the hot, damp greenhouse. Bright geraniums glowed everywhere, and the maidenhair ferns hung cool and green.

Certainly the whistling came from the

greenhouse. The children looked here and there to find what made the noise. And then they found it.

It was made by a small man, who was peeping out of a trap-door under the staging on which the pots stood. He wore a bright green hat on his head, decorated with red cherries as small as peas. In his mouth was a silver whistle and he was blowing this with all his might.

"I say!" said Daniel, in surprise,

staring at him. "Look, Susie! Who's that?"

Susie looked and she couldn't believe her eyes. The man was so tiny, only a little bigger than her biggest doll.

As soon as the little man saw the children looking at him, he took the whistle out of his mouth and beamed at them.

"I thought you'd hear me and come and find out what the noise was," he said. "Snowball, your rabbit, gave me a message for you."

"Snowball gave you a message!" said Daniel, more surprised than ever. "Where is he?"

"I'll tell you about it," said the little man, climbing out of the trap-door and sitting down on an upturned pot nearby. "Last night the Princess of Nowhere came by in her carriage. It was drawn by four black rabbits, and one of them stepped on a spray of bramble and hurt his foot in your garden. So the coachman hunted about for another rabbit to take his place, and of course he saw Snowball."

"And did they take Snowball?" asked Susie, her eyes wide open in astonishment.

"Yes," said the little man. "He didn't want to go, because it is difficult to get back from the Land of Nowhere, and the Princess Juliana might want to keep him, if he pulled her carriage well. So he was sad to have to go. And he called out a message to me as he went galloping off with the three black rabbits. He said, 'Please tell Susie and Daniel where I'm going, and if I'm not back by the time two days and two nights have passed, ask them to come and fetch me.'"

"Goodness me!" cried Daniel, hardly able to believe such a strange tale. "Is it true? Has Snowball really gone to the Land of Nowhere? Where is it?"

"I don't know," said the little man, shaking his head. "But if I were you I'd wait till tomorrow night, and then if he isn't back by midnight, I should go and look for him if you love him very much."

"Yes, we do love him very much," said Susie. "But suppose he doesn't come back, how can we find him?"

"I'll help you all I can," said the little man. "If he's not back, come and rap on my trap-door and I'll open it. Come just after midnight."

"Oh thank you!" said the two children. "We will!"

The little man waved goodbye, climbed

into the hole, and shut the trap-door down. The children went out of the greenhouse, excited and puzzled. It was all so strange.

They waited all that day and night and all the next day for Snowball. But he didn't come back. They went to bed on the second evening, and kept awake till midnight. Then they crept downstairs to see if Snowball was back in his hutch; but he wasn't.

"Well, we'll have to go and look for him," said Daniel. "Are you afraid, Susie?"

"Not a bit," said Susie. "I love Snowball too much to be afraid. Besides, I'll have you to look after me, Daniel."

"Well, come on, we'll go and rap on the trap-door," said Daniel. The moon was shining brightly as they went into the greenhouse. Both children had quickly slipped on their clothes before they had gone down to the garden, just in *case* they might have to go and look for Snowball, so they were quite ready.

The trap-door was fast closed. Daniel could hardly see where it was. At last

he found it and rapped on it. At first nothing happened – and then, when he rapped more loudly a second time, it suddenly flew open and the little man looked out.

"Hallo, hallo, hallo!" he said. "I was quite expecting you. So Snowball hasn't come back?"

"No," said Daniel. "And we're going to look for him and bring him back. You said you'd help us."

"I can't help you much, I'm afraid," said the little man. "But I'll take you to someone who *might* be able to help you a lot. Come down through the trap-door."

"We can't," said Daniel. "We're too big!"

"Nonsense!" said the little man, with a laugh. "Try and see!"

Daniel put his foot through the trap-door – and goodness me, what a surprise! He suddenly grew as small as the little man, and found it was quite easy to squeeze through the trap-door. He looked up at Susie. She seemed enormous and she was gazing at him in the greatest astonishment.

"Come on, Susie!" called Daniel. "It's all right!"

So Susie put *her* foot into the trap-door

30

and she too shot down small – as small as one of her dolls. She was so surprised.

"The greenhouse looks enormous!" she said, looking round. "I say, Daniel, isn't this an adventure!"

"Come on," said the little man. "We haven't much time to spare. What are your names? Mine is Squiddle."

"What a funny name!" said Susie, laughing. "Mine's Susie, and this is Daniel."

"What peculiar names!" said Squiddle, laughing too. "I've never heard them before – but Squiddle is quite a common name in Fairyland."

"Are you a fairy, then?" asked Daniel excited.

"Well, not exactly," said Squiddle. "I'm half a goblin and half a pixie. But I belong to the fairy folk and know them all. Come along, down this passage, and mind the step at the end."

Along they all went, and soon came to a big door with a lamp hanging over it. On the door was a brass plate on which a name was written – Mr Spectacles.

"Mr Spectacles!" said Daniel laughing.

"Another funny name!"

Squiddle knocked at the door and it opened. A tall, thin man peered out, and Daniel and Susie saw why he had such a peculiar name. He wore three pairs of spectacles! One was at the end of his nose, one was on the bridge of his nose and the third pair was up on his forehead.

"What do you want?" asked Mr Spectacles, in a gruff voice.

"Oh, Mr Spectacles, could you help these two children?" asked Squiddle. "They want to go to the Land of Nowhere, and they don't know where it is. You know so much, and you have so many clever books to tell you everything you want to know. Could you tell them which way to go?"

"Come in and sit down," said Mr Spectacles, smiling a sudden smile at the two shy children. "I'll see what I can do."

Daniel and Susie sat down in two big armchairs. Squiddle sat down on a stool. The children stared and stared at funny Mr Spectacles and his three pairs of glasses. They longed to know

why he wore so many pairs at once.

"I'll help you on one condition," said Mr Spectacles, putting a fourth pair of spectacles on his nose. "And that is that you don't ask me why I wear so many pairs of spectacles. I'm so tired of answering that question."

Daniel and Susie were very glad they hadn't asked it.

"We shouldn't dream of asking you things you didn't want to tell us," said Daniel, politely. "But please *could* you tell us where the Land of Nowhere is?"

"Well, it might be Anywhere!" said Mr

Spectacles. "Yes, it might be Anywhere!"

"Well, could you tell us where Anywhere is and we'll go and look there," said Susie.

"Yes, I'll tell you where Anywhere is," said Mr Spectacles, and he took down a great big atlas with many strange maps in it. He poked his finger here and there and at last pointed to an island in the middle of a yellow sea.

"Anywhere is on the island at the moment," he said. "It's a strange land, you know; it moves about from place to place. Well, Nowhere might possibly be

in the middle of Anywhere. So I should advise you to look there."

"How can we get there?" asked Susie.

"Take the train to Golden Sands, and catch the boat to the Island of Anywhere," said Mr Spectacles, taking off the fourth pair of spectacles and polishing them with his handkerchief. "But mind you catch the boat – there's only one goes every week, and that's tomorrow."

"But can we travel all night?" asked Daniel.

"It's daytime in Fairyland, so you'll

be all right," said Mr Spectacles. "Off you go now, and catch the train. And thanks very much for not asking about my spectacles!"

"I'll go with you," said Squiddle, taking the children by the hands. "I'd like to help you."

So Daniel and Susie and the little man in the green hat went out of the door and into the passage again. Squiddle hurried them up some steps and they suddenly came to what looked like a tiny room with a seat in it. Squiddle pushed the children down on the seat and pulled a rope hanging down nearby.

"Oooooooh!" gasped the children – for the little room was a lift and it shot up tremendously quickly, quite taking away their breaths. It rose up for about three minutes and at last came to a stop on a very high hill.

"Get out," said Squiddle. "The lift's going down again."

They walked out of the lift and watched it sink swiftly down into the hill, out of sight. Then they looked round. What a long way they could see!

The hill was very, very steep, and as slippery as glass. Nobody could possibly climb up or down it. Just behind them, resting on the shoulders of the hill, was a long bank of cloud. It stayed quite still and didn't move at all, as clouds usually do.

"Where's the train?" asked Susie. "Surely there can't possibly be a railway on this hill!"

"It's a cloud railway," explained Squiddle. "You wait a minute and you'll see the train! It's due very soon."

Almost as he spoke there came the rattle of wheels, and to the children's great delight they saw the prettiest train imaginable running along the bank of cloud just near them. It was the colour of the blue sky, and each carriage was in the shape of a bird.

"How does it go?" asked Daniel. "Does it go by steam?"

"No, by lightning," said Squiddle. "You'll see how quickly it goes when you're in it."

They all climbed into a carriage that was shaped like a kingfisher. The engine-driver, a goblin with a funny apple-like face, leaned out to see that they

were safely in, and then off they went, running along the clouds in the sky.

The train went so very fast that both children clutched hold of the sides of the car and had to gasp for breath.

"Oh, goodness!" said Daniel, when at last he could speak. "It certainly does go like lightning!"

It was a wonderful ride. It was bright daylight, just as Mr Spectacles had said, and the children had a marvellous view of their world as they travelled swiftly along the clouds on the strange, airy railway. Then they came to Fairyland

and saw the beautiful spires, towers and pinnacles of that dream-like land. They wished the journey would never end, as they travelled along the clouds that hung over Fairyland.

"I hope we shall catch the boat to Anywhere," said Squiddle, suddenly, looking anxiously at a very large red watch. "The train's not so fast as usual. There was a big storm last night and some of the lightning got used up, so there's not so much for the train today."

"Oh my, I hope we shall be in time," said Susie in dismay. "Mr Spectacles said there was only one boat a week."

On went the train and on, and at last the children cried out that they could see the sea.

"Then we're nearly there," said Squiddle, looking at his watch again. "I hope my watch is fast."

The train came to a standstill on a cloud that rested on another very high hill. Out jumped Squiddle and the children and rushed to a lift that stood waiting. They got into it, Squiddle pulled the rope and down they shot at such a speed that Susie really thought she was falling and cried out in fright.

The lift stopped at the bottom and the three of them ran out. They found themselves on a beach where the sand was as bright as gold.

"This is Golden Sands," said Squiddle. "Oh dear, where's the boat?"

"There it is!" cried Daniel, pointing. "It's gone!"

Sure enough it had! It was far out to sea, a big boat with yellow sails. "We're too late," said Squiddle, sadly. "We're too late. Now what shall we do? Can you possibly wait a week? Then you could catch the next boat."

"No, we couldn't possibly," said

Daniel. "Why, our mother would worry terribly if we didn't go home."

"Oh, we must, we *must* rescue Snowball," said Susie, with tears in her eyes. "Oh, Squiddle, can't you think of something?"

Squiddle shook his head. Susie began to cry properly and Daniel and Squiddle took out their handkerchiefs and tried to comfort her. She wouldn't be comforted and she made such a noise that Daniel was quite upset.

"What's the matter with the little girl?" asked a surprised voice, suddenly. Daniel looked up and saw a mermaid

sitting on a rock, her tail in a warm pool.

"We've missed the boat and don't know how to get to Anywhere." he said, sadly.

"Why don't you fly?" asked the mermaid, beginning to comb out her hair. "Mother Dibble has a fine lot of gulls' wings to lend to people who miss the boat. She only charges a penny a time."

"Where does Mother Dibble live?" asked Squiddle.

"In that cave over there," said the mermaid, pointing. The children turned and saw a cave nearby, with a little gate in front of it.

"Oh, we'll go and get some wings, then," said Squiddle, gladly. He took the children's hands and they went over to the cave. Mother Dibble was sitting in it, sewing. All around her hung beautiful wings, grey, white and black.

"Good-day, Mother Dibble," said Squiddle, politely. "Would you lend us three pairs of gulls' wings, please? We have missed the boat and we want to get to the Island of Anywhere at once. Here are three pennies for the wings."

Mother Dibble took the pennies, and then chose three pairs of pearly-grey wings. She fastened them carefully to their shoulders. The children felt most

excited. They had often flown in dreams, but never in real life, and they could hardly wait until their wings were safely on.

"Spread them out well, and fly slowly," said Mother Dibble.

They spread their wings and flapped them – and at once they rose up into the air! It was glorious. The children flew strongly over the water, and in a little while they had passed right over the ship they had missed.

"We shall be there before the ship!" cried Daniel. "Oh, look, Squiddle – is that the Island of Anywhere?"

"Yes," said Squiddle. "Isn't it strange?"

It was indeed a strange island, for it

changed its shape as they watched it. It seemed alive. In the centre of it was a shining town, whose towers gleamed like gold.

"Ah, that's the Land of Nowhere," said Squiddle, pleased. "Mr Spectacles said it might be Anywhere and so it is! It's in the middle of the island, so we are sure to find your rabbit, Snowball, there. Hurray!"

They all flew down into the shining town. "We had better go the palace and ask for the stables," said Squiddle. So he stopped a hurrying gnome and asked the way to the palace of the Princess Juliana. Then on they went, their big gulls' wings folded neatly behind them.

They came to the glittering palace and

walked a little way round it, to where the stables were. Squiddle pushed open a door in the wall and they passed through it into the stables. Rabbits were kept there, all jet-black and beautiful. Their whiskers were carefully curled each morning and their ears were brushed. The children couldn't see their white rabbit, Snowball, anywhere. They asked a servant where he was.

"Oh, the Princess Juliana likes him so much that she has made him her pet," said the little servant. "He is sitting on a black velvet cushion by her knee, in the palace."

"Goodness! Now we shall have to go and ask her for him," said Squiddle. "That may be awkward. Listen, children – if the Princess is unkind and won't let Snowball go, wait for a signal from me. Then, as soon as you see me wink hard at you, snatch up Snowball and run to the window. Fly out and up into the sky as quickly as you can. I'll stay behind to stop the Princess from sending her flying-gnomes after you."

Feeling most excited the children

went with Squiddle to the palace gates. They went through them and made their way into the palace. They asked a servant to take them to the Princess, and when at last they came to where she was sitting, they saw, to their great joy, their lovely rabbit, Snowball, sitting on a cushion at her feet, looking very bored and unhappy.

"Oh Snowball!" cried Susie, joyfully, and she ran to him and hugged him. "Oh, Your Highness, this is my darling bunny! You borrowed him the other night when one of your rabbits went lame, but now I have come to fetch him home again."

The Princess Juliana was very beautiful and spoilt. She shook her curly golden head and looked cross.

"He is my pet now," she said. "You can't have him. You shall have a sack of gold instead."

"No, I want my rabbit," said Susie, firmly. The Princess cried out crossly and ran to ring a big bell near the fireplace. "I will tell my servants to turn you out of the palace," she cried,

angrily. "You shan't have Snowball."

Squiddle winked hard at Susie and Daniel. They knew it was a signal to act at once, so Daniel picked up the rabbit in his arms, and Susie ran to the window and opened it. In a second the children spread out their wings and were up in the air! Squiddle was left behind to stop the Princess from sending servants after them.

Over the sea flew Daniel and Susie, leaving the strange Land of Nowhere, set in the Island of Anywhere, far behind them. They wondered if Squiddle was all right – and then, to their great delight, they heard the swish-swish of big wings and there he was, flying beside them once more!

"I couldn't stop the Princess from sending out her flying gnomes!" he cried breathlessly. "We mustn't stop at Golden Sands, for there is no train to take us away. We must fly straight on!"

Daniel and Susie looked behind and saw a whole crowd of little gnomes flying swiftly through the air after them. They

flapped their gulls' wings all the faster and soon the gnomes were left behind. On went the children, and on and on, Daniel carrying the frightened rabbit carefully in his arms, and Squiddle keeping a look-out for the gnomes.

"Fly down to earth now," he said, suddenly. So down they flew and landed in a garden – and whatever do you think? It was their very own garden, and there was the greenhouse just nearby! They had flown all the way home! As they dropped downwards the daylight disappeared, and when they stood on the ground, everywhere was dark save for

faint, shining moonlight. It was night-time again, as soon as they had left Fairyland behind!

"Put Snowball into his hutch and get back to bed quickly," said Squiddle to the children. "You'll still be able to get a little sleep. Leave your gulls' wings in the garden. They will fly back to Mother Dibble by themselves."

Daniel put Snowball safely back into his hutch. Then the children said a loving goodnight to him, and you should have seen how his nose twitched with delight to be safely home again! Then they carefully took off their wings and put them on the grass. Just as they turned to go indoors they heard a swishing sound – and hey presto, the wings rose up by themselves and flew away! It was very strange.

"Goodbye, goodbye," whispered Squiddle, pressing their hands. "I'm glad I was able to help you. Come and see me again sometimes."

"Oh, we will!" said the children. "Goodbye and thank you so much!"

They crept into bed, surprised to find

themselves their own size once more.

"What an adventure, Susie!" said Daniel, as he put his head down on his pillow. "It's all mixed up in my mind – the cross Princess, the Island of Anywhere, Mother Dibble and the mermaid, the Cloud Railway and that funny old Mr Spectacles!"

"I *wish* we knew why he wore so many

spectacles!" sighed Susie. "That's just one thing I really *would* like to know!"

I'd like to know too, wouldn't you? But I don't expect we shall ever know!

Staying with
Auntie Sue

"Where are we going to for our holidays this summer, Mummy?" asked Katie. "I want to go to the seaside again – the same place as last year."

"Daddy and I are going away by ourselves for a change, dear," said her mother. "I feel rather tired, and want to be just with Daddy."

"But what's to happen to *me*?" cried Katie, in dismay. "*I* want to come too."

"No, Katie," said Daddy. "You're going to stay with your Auntie Sue. You haven't behaved very well lately, and Mummy and I are afraid we've spoilt you. I think it will do Mummy good to leave you with someone else for a little while – you really are growing selfish and rude, you know!"

Katie was quite horrified. She was

an only child, and she *had* been spoilt. Mummy was far too easy with her, and now Katie had grown into a most unpleasant little girl.

"I don't like Auntie Sue," said Katie. "She doesn't like me either."

"Oh yes she does," said her mother, who simple couldn't imagine anyone not liking her beautiful, precious Katie. "She will be very nice to you indeed."

So Katie went to stay with Auntie Sue. She wasn't very nice to her aunt. "I wanted to go with Mummy and Daddy," she said. "I didn't want to come and stay with you!"

"Well, I'm afraid you'll have to put up with me, Katie!" said her aunt, cheerfully. "I hope you'll help me, and will like the things I cook for you."

But Katie was quite determined she wouldn't help, and wouldn't like anything at all! Making her stay with Auntie Sue when she wanted to go to the seaside!

So she wouldn't run a single errand. She turned up her pretty little nose at treacle pudding and at ginger cake. She even stamped her foot at her aunt. What she really wanted, of course, was a good slap, but Auntie Sue knew that Katie's mother would never forgive her if she slapped her.

"I hope you don't behave like this at home, Katie," said her aunt. "I don't wonder your mother needs a holiday without you, if you do. You seem to expect to do everything that you like, and nothing that you don't!"

"That's a good idea," said Katie. "I shall go to bed when I like, I shall get up when I like, I shall wear what clothes I like, and I shall *DO* just what I like!"

She expected her auntie to be very upset and cross, and to argue with her. But Auntie Sue gave a little laugh, looked up from her sewing, and said: "Very well, Katie. I won't bother about you, if you feel like that. Do what you please!"

"Good!" thought Katie. "That's fine." So that night she stayed up until ten o'clock. Think of it! Ten o'clock, when all children should have been in bed for a long, long time.

Auntie Sue said nothing at all. At ten she put her book away, said good

night to Katie, and went upstairs. Katie thought she would stay up even later, but somehow the house seemed too empty and quiet. So she went up to bed.

In the morning she overslept herself, of course, for she was very tired. She awoke about half-past nine, scrambled into her clothes, and went downstairs to breakfast.

But there wasn't any. "I've had mine," said Auntie Sue. "I always have it at quarter-past eight. I've cleared away and washed up, because I have to go out and do the shopping."

So Katie had no breakfast, and she was very cross indeed. Auntie Sue went out with her shopping bag. Katie went to the larder. But it was locked! So she couldn't get anything to eat. Bother, bother, bother!

She was very naughty at dinner-time. She ate with her arms on the table, and spilt gravy and fruit-juice down the front of her dress.

"It doesn't matter," she said. "I'll put on my best dress this afternoon. Then you can wash this one, Auntie Sue!"

"I shan't have time," said Auntie Sue. So she didn't wash the dirty dress. Katie put on her best blue velvet one. Then she did something she knew she shouldn't do in her very best dress.

She got out her plasticine and her paint-box and began playing with them. "You know you have an overall, don't you?" said Auntie Sue.

"'Course I do," said Katie, "but I want to play like this." When teatime came you should have seen Katie's dress! It was splashed with paint, and had marks all over it where she had wiped the plasticine off her fingers. It was quite spoilt.

Auntie Sue called her to tea. "I can't

come till I've finished my picture,"
answered Katie rudely.

And, oh dear, when at last she did
go to tea, that was all cleared away
too, just as breakfast had been. Katie
stamped and yelled, but Auntie Sue took
no notice.

"You do what you like, and there is no

reason why I should not do the same," she said, sewing quietly. "Stop shouting or you will upset Tinker."

Tinker was the cat. He didn't like Katie at all, because she pulled his tail. Katie gave another terrific yell, and Tinker flew at her. He dug his claws into her arm, and gave her a line of red scratches. Then Katie yelled in earnest.

"Tinker is going to do what *he* likes too," said Auntie Sue. "You'd better bathe your arm. It isn't very nice, is it,

Katie, when we do what we like, and don't bother about one another? But you have chosen that way of behaving, and I will choose it too. So will Tinker."

At half-past six Auntie Sue looked at the clock. "Will you go and turn on the gas under the little saucepan in the kitchen?" she said.

"No," said Katie, who wasn't going to do a single thing if she could help it. Auntie Sue said nothing. She didn't go out to the kitchen to turn on the gas either.

"I'm hungry," said Katie at last. "I've

had no tea. I want something to eat."

"Well, I did tell you to turn on the gas under the little saucepan in the kitchen," said Auntie Sue. "I was going to cook you an egg. But I shan't bother now, as *you* didn't bother."

"I will bother, I will!" said Katie, suddenly feeling hungry enough to eat a dozen eggs. She flew out to the kitchen and lit the gas.

She boiled the egg herself, cut some bread and butter, and had it for her supper. Then she actually went up to bed. But her bed was not made, and the room was dusty and untidy.

She rushed downstairs. "Auntie Sue!

You forgot to make my bed! And my room's terrible."

"Put it right, then," said Auntie Sue. "And if you want your bed made, make it yourself. I am doing what I like, remember, just as you are – and I *don't* like making your bed or doing your room."

Katie was angry and shouted. But Auntie Sue took no notice. Tinker suddenly stood up – and Katie fled. She wasn't going to be scratched by that horrid, bad-tempered cat again!

She was down to breakfast in good time the next morning. She had on another clean dress, her last clean one, for she had only brought three with her.

"Hadn't you better put on your overall, as that is your last clean dress?" asked Auntie Sue. "*I* don't mind, of course, but you might possibly want a clean dress some time."

"I don't like my overall," said Katie, "and I don't *want* to put it on."

And at breakfast-time what did she do but spill her cocoa all down the front of her clean dress!

Auntie Sue didn't say a word. Katie dried her dress as best she could. She rather wished she *had* had on her overall, but she wasn't going to say so. Oh, dear me, no!

That afternoon the little girl next door came to say she was having a small party, and would Auntie Sue's niece Katie like to come too?

"Oh *yes*," said Katie. "I *love* parties!"

When the little girl had gone, Katie spoke to her aunt in rather a meek voice. "Auntie, all my dresses are dirty. I do

like to look nice when I go to a party. Will you wash one for me?"

"I shall have my sewing-meeting here today," said Auntie Sue. "I shall have no time."

"But, Auntie – I can't go to a party in a dirty dress!" said Katie, almost in tears.

"No, you can't possibly," Auntie agreed. "You could go in your overall. You haven't worn it, so it's still clean."

"I *can't* go to a party in an overall!" cried Katie, horrified. "I can't. Everyone would laugh at me."

"It might do you good to be laughed at," said Auntie Sue. "Maybe you wouldn't be so careless with your dresses then. Well, do as you like. Wear your overall and go – or don't wear it, and stay at home."

Katie didn't go, and she sat listening sulkily to all the fun going on next door. She didn't even like to go to see her auntie's sewing friends, because her dress was so dirty. So she went without her tea.

It wasn't much fun doing exactly as she liked if Auntie did the same. Katie

was bored, so she made her bed and tidied her room. She felt pleased when she saw how nice it looked. She thought she would go out into the garden and get a few flowers to put in her room. Auntie had said she might, but she hadn't bothered to.

She went out and picked some. Then she picked some for her aunt's bedroom, too! She didn't know why she did, except that she felt she would rather like to have a word of praise from Auntie Sue.

It was horrid living with somebody who didn't seem a bit interested in you.

Auntie Sue was very pleased with the flowers. "That was nice of you, Katie," she said. "Now you make me feel *I* want to be nice too. I shall buy tickets for the circus the day after tomorrow!"

But the next day Katie was silly again. She thought she would go for a walk, and off she set, without coat or hat or scarf. Auntie Sue called after her. "It's going to rain. Wouldn't it be best to wear your mackintosh, sou'wester and rubber boots?"

"Don't fuss, Auntie," said Katie, cheekily, and wouldn't go back. So, of course, she got caught in a real storm and was soon wet through. She tried to shelter under a tree, but the wind caught her there, and she shivered with cold.

She ran all the way home in the rain. "You had better get straight into a warm bed," said Auntie Sue, "or you will get a cold."

But Katie wouldn't. She didn't want to. So by the next morning she had a

terrible cold and didn't feel well enough to get out of bed at all.

She wondered if Auntie Sue would think she was oversleeping, and clear away the breakfast things again and go out shopping and leave her. Oh dear, and she felt so bad! It would be nice to have somebody being kind to her. She wouldn't be able to go to the circus now, either! Katie cried into her pillow and felt very sorry for herself.

Auntie Sue came in with a breakfast tray. She straightened the bedclothes, banged the pillows, gave Katie two hankies, brushed her hair, and then set the tray in front of her.

"We can't go to the circus," said Katie,

in a small voice. "I've got such a bad cold. Will the tickets be wasted?"

"My dear child, when I saw you going out yesterday without a mack I knew you would get wet through and have a cold today, so I was not foolish enough to buy the tickets," said Auntie Sue. "Now, if you are going to be sensible and do what you are told, for once, then I shall be sensible and kind, too."

"Oh, I *do* want you to be kind to me

today," begged Katie, and she actually took her aunt's hand. "I've been awfully silly."

"You've been worse than silly," said Auntie Sue, briskly. "You've been horrible. But there – it's not altogether your fault, as I've said before. You've been spoilt!"

Katie did everything she was told. She ate what her aunt brought her, she took her medicines, she had a sleep in the afternoon, and she was patient and grateful and polite.

"Well!" said Auntie Sue, after tea, opening a book to read to Katie. "What a surprise you are, Katie! I'd no idea you had any niceness in you. If I'm not careful I shall end up by liking you very much."

"Oh, do, Auntie!" said Katie. "I *want* you to like me. I'd be proud if you did. I know I'm spoilt, but I'll try not to be with you. I shan't do what I like any more – I'll do what *you* like!"

"We'll *both* do that," said Auntie Sue, pleased, and she opened the book to read to Katie.

She and Katie had a nice time after that – but I don't know what will happen when Katie goes back home to her mother and father. If they spoil her again, it will be hard for her to be nice, won't it? She'd better go and live with Auntie Sue!

The Little Dog
Next Door

"Willie, Miss Little next door has bought a dog," said Mother.

"What sort of dog?" asked Willie.

"Oh, an ordinary sort of dog," said Mother. "Too long a tail, really, and not a long enough nose – but he looks a good-natured little fellow. You should offer to take him out for walks, Willie. Miss Little can't walk very far because of her bad leg."

But Willie didn't like walks very much. He liked to sit and read or do jigsaw puzzles all day long when he wasn't at school.

He had a look at Miss Little's dog. The dog looked at him, and wagged his tail. He had big brown eyes and a solemn, doggy face with little whiskers sticking out each side.

"I don't think much of *you*," said Willie to the dog. "You're a very ordinary-looking dog. And what a silly bark you've got. It's only a yap. I don't like yappy dogs."

The dog wagged his tail again. He didn't understand what Willie was saying, but it was nice to be talked to. He wondered if this boy would take him for a good long walk. Miss Little never did – and the dog did love a walk so much.

Willie had a cat, but he wasn't always

kind to it. He often pulled its tail, and chased it, and the cat always fled when it saw him coming. He had a canary, too, but he couldn't remember to feed it or give it water. His mother had to do that or the little bird would have died. He wasn't kind to Dusty, Miss Little's dog. He threw stones at him! Dusty didn't understand at first, and ran after the stones – and then when some began to hit him and make him yelp he was very upset.

He stood and stared at Willie out of his big, brown eyes. What a strange boy! Why was he so unkind?

All the same, Dusty always wagged his tail hard when he saw Willie coming, and tried to lick his hand. He was a good-natured little dog, always ready to forget an unkindness.

"You're silly," said Willie. "You're ordinary! You have a yap instead of a bark. Your tail is too long and your nose is too short."

Miss Little gave Dusty a ball for himself. He loved it. He rolled it all the way down the garden and back, and then he threw it up into the air and practised catching it. When he saw Willie he ran to him and put the ball down at his feet.

"Play with me!" he barked. "Throw me the ball and see how well I can catch it."

And what do you think Willie did? He threw the ball up into a tree, and there it stayed. Dusty tried his hardest to climb the tree, but he couldn't, of course. He sat at the bottom and yapped forlornly.

"That's a horrid boy," said the cat, who was watching. "When he's gone in I'll climb up the tree and try to get the

ball down for you, Dusty."

But the cat couldn't, because the ball was stuck fast between two branches. So Dusty lost his only plaything and was very sad.

Now, every time Willie went out on an errand for his mother Dusty followed him, hoping for a walk. But Willie always threw stones at him, so he didn't walk near to the boy, he kept a long way behind. Willie felt angry with Dusty for following him, and he hid round corners to jump out at him when he came trotting near.

But all the same Dusty followed him. It was the next-best thing to a walk, following someone, even if he had to keep a long way behind.

One day Willie had to go to the farm for his mother. He decided to go along by the river. Off he went, and Dusty saw him go. He ran out of Miss Little's gate and down the road, keeping a good way behind Willie. But Willie soon saw him, of course, and sent a stone whizzing by him.

Willie climbed over the stile and crossed the field to the river. There was a big white swan there. Well, you can imagine what Willie did! He picked up a stone and threw it at the lovely bird.

And the swan came out of the water after Willie! Yes, it really did. Swans will

do that sometimes, if they are angry, and this one was very angry indeed. It half walked, half flew to Willie, and hit him with one of its great wings.

"Oh! Oh! You've hurt me!" yelled Willie, and he turned to run. The swan pecked at one of his legs with its strong beak, and Willie fell. He rolled over and went into the water, splash!

The swan walked to the bank and looked down into the water. That boy was there, struggling. The swan wondered whether to give him another hard peck or not – but then it saw a little dog coming along, and it slid gracefully into the water and swam off.

The little dog was Dusty, of course. He had been a long way behind Willie, and he had wondered what the swan was doing when it came out of the water.

Then he saw Willie fall and disappear over the bank. Now he was peeping over into the water, wondering what had happened to the boy.

Willie was yelling and shouting! He was struggling hard. "Save me! Save me! Help, help, I'm drowning! Save me!"

Dusty didn't stop to think. He threw himself into the water and swam to Willie. He caught hold of his coat as the boy was sinking under the water. He tugged at him and tried to pull him towards the bank.

At last he got the boy there. Willie felt sand beneath his feet and struggled out of the river, sobbing with fright.

He managed to get up on the bank, and lay there, panting. He looked at his leg. It was bleeding where the swan had pecked it so savagely. His arm hurt too, where the swan had hit it with its wing.

Dusty licked him timidly and sat down beside him, looking at him kindly out of his big, brown eyes.

"Oh, Dusty!" said Willie. "You saved me. I was drowning."

"Wuff," said Dusty, and licked him again.

"I'll see if I can walk," said Willie. "But I don't think I can. That swan pecked me so very hard. It's damaged my leg. I can't stand on it."

He sank down to the grass again. He wasn't a very brave little boy, and he cried bitterly because he was wet and hurt and frightened, and there was nobody but Dusty to comfort him.

Still, Dusty was a very great comfort indeed. He sat close to Willie. He licked his tears away. He nuzzled against him kindly as if to say, "Cheer up! I'll stay with you. I'm your friend."

Willie put his arms round the little dog. Dusty was surprised and delighted. The boy pressed his cheek against Dusty's soft head.

"Dusty! How can you be so kind to me when I've always been so horrid to you? Why don't you bite me and run away? Why did you jump into the water and save me?"

Dusty looked at him out of faithful doggy eyes and wagged his tail. He liked being hugged by Willie. He was a loving, kind little dog and he wanted people to be the same.

"Dusty! I'll never forget how kind and forgiving you are," said Willie. "I'm sorry I was horrid to you. Will you forget it and be my friend?"

Dusty wagged his tail so hard that it wagged his body, too. Dear me, how very nice Willie was! He licked him again.

Willie began to shiver. He was wet and cold, the wind was strong on the river bank, and the sun had gone in. "I wish somebody would come," said Willie.

"I haven't even got a hanky to bind up my leg."

Dusty understood. He wriggled out of Willie's arms. He would go and fetch somebody to help Willie. At first the boy didn't understand. He thought Dusty was leaving him. Then suddenly he understood.

"You're going to fetch someone to help me! Clever dog! Good Dog!"

Dusty sped off to Willie's home. He ran in at the door and found Willie's mother. He pulled at her skirt. She looked down, surprised. Dusty ran to the door and stood there, wagging his tail.

Then he ran back to her and pulled her skirt again.

"Dusty! What's the matter? Why do you want me to go with you?" said Willie's mother, puzzled. "Surely – surely nothing has happened to Willie?"

Dusty ran to the gate and back, trying to tell Willie's mother that she must come. She ran out and followed. Dusty took her across the field to the river bank – and there was poor Willie, still sitting there, shivering, his leg giving him a lot of pain.

His mother helped him home, alarmed and sorry. Dusty trotted beside them, licking Willie's hand when he could. Willie told his mother all that the brave little dog had done. His mother patted

Dusty's head, and he barked in delight.

"You shall have the biggest bone I've got when I've put Willie to bed and bandaged his leg," she said. "Oh, Willie – that horrid swan. I shall see about having it destroyed."

Willie went red. "No, Mother," he said. "It was my fault. Everything was my fault. I threw a stone at the swan."

"Oh, Willie!" said his mother. "I wish you wouldn't be so unkind to birds and animals."

"Mother, I'm never going to be again," said Willie. "Listen – I was as unkind as I could be to little Dusty, here – I threw stones at him, too – I threw his only ball up into the tree – I teased him – I wouldn't let him come for walks with me."

"And yet he jumped into the river and saved you, and sat by to comfort you, and fetched me to help you," said his mother. "Oh, Willie!"

"Yes – I'm horrid," said Willie. "Mother, it isn't nice to think that a dog is better than a boy – but Dusty's much, much better than I am – kind and

forgiving and loving. I'm ashamed."

"Are you, Willie?" said his mother. "Well, there's hope for you then! I'll just see how you behave when your leg is better and you're up again."

Would you like to know what Willie did when his leg was better? He climbed the tree and got Dusty's ball down. He emptied his money-box and bought him a bag of biscuits, an enormous bone and a new collar. And he did something that Dusty liked even better than that.

He took him for a long, long walk every day. I know, because they pass my

house there and back, and I often hear Willie saying something that Dusty likes very much.

"Best dog in the world, aren't you?" he says.

And Dusty says, "Wuff, wuff, wuff, wuff, wuff" – which means, "And you're the best boy!"

On Jimmy's Birthday

Jimmy was looking forward to his birthday. Mummy always gave the children a lovely time then. She had promised Jimmy a party, with a big cake and candles. She had bought boxes of crackers and put them away.

Jimmy told Jill about them, and about the cake Mummy was going to make. Jill was his sister, and she was looking forward to Jimmy's birthday.

"Baby is too little to know about birthdays yet," said Jimmy. "He's only had one birthday and that was the day he was born. I hope he won't mind the crackers popping off."

Then something sad happened. The day before Jimmy's birthday Baby fell ill. Mummy was very worried and she called in the doctor.

"You must keep the baby very, very quiet," said the doctor, looking grave. "Don't let the others bother him or make a noise. He must sleep all he can."

After the doctor had gone Mummy spoke to Jimmy and Jill. "I'm sorry, dears," she said, "but I'm afraid that as Baby is so ill we must put off the party tomorrow. It would be too noisy – and the crackers would frighten him, poor mite."

Jimmy was dreadfully disappointed. Birthdays and birthday parties only came once a year, and on birthdays you couldn't help feeling happy and noisy.

Now he and Jill would have to creep about, and not laugh loudly, nor even have anyone in the house.

"Be brave about it, Jimmy," said Mummy, seeing how sad both children looked. "I'm so worried about Baby. You must help me, if you can, and we'll have the party when Baby is better."

Jimmy put his arms around his mother. "Don't you worry about my birthday!" he said, and he tried to smile. "That doesn't matter a bit!"

But it did matter, of course, and when his birthday morning came, and Mummy was too worried about Baby to make a fuss of him, Jimmy felt very sad. He had to go round to all his friends and tell them not to come to the party. On the way back Jill and Jimmy met old Mr Benny. He was carrying a basket full of shopping which looked much too heavy for him.

Jimmy ran up to him and took the basket. "I'll carry it," he said. "We are going your way."

"Thank you, thank you!" said old Mr Benny, twinkling his blue eyes at them.

"You're always such a well-mannered boy, Jimmy. Now – let me see – surely it is your birthday today! Are you having a party?"

Then Jimmy told him about Baby being so ill, and Mr Benny listened and nodded. "So I'm not really keeping my birthday today," said Jimmy.

"But I can't have a birthday wasted

like that!" said Mr Benny. "*I'll* have a party for you!"

"Oh, Mr Benny – but your house is much too small for a party!" said Jimmy. And indeed Mr Benny's cottage was only just big enough to take him and his old black cat!

"I won't have it at my house!" said Mr Benny. "I'll have it at the Zoo! I'll hire a big car and we'll take you and your friends in it to the Zoo! Yes, and we'll take your birthday cake and crackers, too, and have them on the lawn there. We can buy lemonade and sandwiches and buns!"

"Oh – do you really mean it?" said Jill and Jimmy together.

"Of course. Go round to your friends again and tell them to come to my house at half-past two," said Mr Benny. "And you bring your cake and crackers!"

So off they all went to the Zoo that afternoon, chattering and laughing in the big car that Mr Benny had ordered.

"Going to the Zoo is an even bigger birthday treat than a party!" said Jimmy, happily. And it was! They saw all the animals, and they gave the monkeys bananas and oranges, and Mr Benny gave the keeper a tin of treacle for the

brown bears. What fun it was to see them licking out the treacle, grunting with joy all the time.

"They're enjoying Jimmy's birthday too!" said Jill and everyone laughed.

Then they had a lovely picnic and ate the birthday cake up, every scrap. It was most delicious. They drank lemonade and orangeade, and then Mr Benny said it was quite time that they all had a ride on the elephants.

Nobody wanted to go home. "Well, of course, you can stay here if you like, and be shut up with the monkeys at closing-time," said Mr Benny, smiling. "But I think you'd better come home with me, really,"

Jimmy and Jill thanked the kind old man for the birthday treat. "It's a pleasure to do anything for well-mannered children!" said old Mr Benny. "I've enjoyed it all too!"

Whey they got home Mummy met them with a smiling face. "Baby's much better! He slept all day long. I'm so glad you had such a happy birthday, Jimmy. You did deserve it, and now you've still got your party to look forward to, haven't you?"

He's having it tomorrow – and he's asking Mr Benny, of course. Have a good time, Jimmy!

Oranges
in the Road

Alan, Mary, Tom, Harry and Lucy were all going home from school one morning when a green van passed them. It bumped over a big hole in the road, and the back door of the van flew open.

Out came a great many oranges, flying out like a lot of balls! They landed in the road near the children and rolled here, there and everywhere.

The children gave squeals of surprise. "Look! Oranges!" shouted Alan.

"Heaps of them!" cried Mary.

"All over the place!" said Tom, and ran to pick one up. "Here's a beauty!"

"Let's pick them up quickly!" said Lucy. "Before anyone else comes along and sees them."

They picked them all up, and then ran to the pavement. "How many are there?"

asked Harry.

"One, two, three – how many have you got, Mary – four, five – I've got one – six how many more? Seven, eight, nine, ten! Ten oranges!"

"How many of us are there?" said Lucy.

"Five," said Tom. "That's two each. Two lovely big oranges each. What a bit of luck."

"Shall we eat them now?" asked Lucy. "I'm hungry, and they look so nice and juicy."

"Yes, let's," said Tom. "I could manage both of mine before we get home."

99

"I don't think we *can* keep them for ourselves," said Mary, in rather a small voice.

All the others turned and looked at her. "Why ever not?" said Lucy. "Finding is always keeping. My mother said so."

"Then she's wrong," said Mary. "If you know who owns the lost thing, you can't possibly keep it. You have to take it back."

"But we don't know the owner!" said Tom. "Aha, Miss Goody – what do you say to that?"

Mary hated going against all the others. She didn't at all like being called Miss Goody. She went very red and wondered if she should say any more.

'I mustn't be a coward,' she thought. 'I simply must speak up!' So she spoke again.

"Well, *I* saw the name on the van. And it was Simpson's, the greengrocer. They're *his* oranges. And I guess the man driving the van will get into trouble when he gets back with ten oranges missing."

"I never thought of that," said Harry, at once. "You're right, Mary. We can't let anyone else be blamed for the missing oranges. Anyway, I know the man who drives the van, and I like him."

"I agree with Harry," said Alan. "If we know the owner, we must take back the oranges. I don't want to be dishonest."

"Pooh!" said Tom. "Who'd know, anyway?"

"*We'd* know!" said Alan. "*I* don't want

to think I'm a thief, thank you. You're my cousin, Tom – I wouldn't want to think *you* were a thief. Come on – let's go and take the oranges back to Simpson's. It's not far."

"Well, *I'm* not going to!" said Lucy, in a temper. "Just when we found them, too! I think you're all silly."

She threw her oranges down on the pavement and ran off, sulking. Harry picked them up.

"Who passes Simpson's?" he said. "You do, don't you, Mary? So do I. We'll take them back between us. Come on.

I'm glad we've done the decent thing."

They said goodbye to the others and went on their way. They came to Simpson's and looked for the man who drove the van. But he wasn't there. Mr Simpson was there himself, a big, burly man with twinkling eyes. He wore a dark-blue apron, and was busy weighing out potatoes.

"Please, Mr Simpson," said Harry, "these oranges fell out of your van when it passed us. Mary saw it was your van so we thought we'd bring them back."

"Well, if that isn't kind of you!" said Mr Simpson, warmly. "I take that very

kindly indeed. Of course, I know both your mothers, so I can guess why they've got good children. Did you know that good mothers have fine children? Well, they do. And the other way round! *Some* children would have kept these oranges for themselves."

"I know," said Mary, remembering Lucy, and remembering too that Lucy hadn't got a very nice mother. "Goodbye, Mr Simpson. We must get home to lunch."

"Wait a minute, wait a minute!" said big Mr Simpson. "You're not the only people that can be kind. Give me a chance, too. Now – how many children are there in your class at school?"

"Twenty-eight," said Harry.

"Right," said Mr Simpson. "Twenty-nine oranges will be delivered at your school this afternoon – one extra for your teacher, you see – and I hope you'll each eat one when you have your ten minutes' play."

"Oh, *thank* you!" said Mary and Harry, together. Their faces shone. Oranges for everyone in the class!

How lovely!

"I'll pick out my best and juiciest," said Mr Simpson.

He did. When his man arrived that afternoon with a big box of oranges, they were the biggest and juiciest the children had ever seen. Miss Brown, their teacher, was most surprised. A note came with them: "For the children of Miss Brown's class with best wishes from T. T. Simpson."

"*Why* has he sent these?" wondered Miss Brown.

Alan told her. "It's really all because of Mary," he said. "Some oranges bounced out of a passing van and we picked them up. We were going to eat them when Mary said she had seen the name on the van. So she and Harry took them back."

"And now Mr Simpson has sent an orange for every single person in the class!" said Miss Brown.

"There's one for you too," said Harry.

"Well, you gave up the oranges you found, and gained an orange for everyone here!" said Miss Brown. "What a wonderful thing! Mary, come up here and give them out. It's because of you we've got them."

So Mary gave out the oranges, and everyone took them with a delighted smile – except one child.

Well, you know who that was, of course. I don't need to say her name. She came up and took her orange, but she didn't smile. She looked away, because she was ashamed.

As for the oranges, they were just about the nicest the children had ever had. Wasn't it a lovely surprise!

Peppermint Rock

Sue and Robin were down at the seaside for the day. Their aunt had asked them to go, and they were very pleased indeed.

"Now, listen," said their mother, as she put on their clean sweaters. "I don't want you to quarrel *once* when you are at your auntie's. Not *once*. You quarrel all day long here, and I don't want Auntie Ellen to hear it."

"It's not me that quarrels, it's Robin," said Sue. "He always begins it."

"Oooh, you fibber!" said Robin. "I would never quarrel at all if you weren't so bad-tempered and cross."

"*Me* bad-tempered!" cried Sue. "Well! I never heard such –"

"There you go again," said their mother. "You can never open your mouths without squabbling. I'll be glad to be rid of you for a day – and that's not a nice thing for a mother to have to say."

She saw them off to the bus that took them to the sea. They squabbled all the way down, but they remembered what their mother had said, when they met their aunt. They were quite nice and polite to one another for once!

They met their big cousin Jim. They didn't like him very much, because he laughed at them.

"Hello, squabblers!" he said. "Learnt to like one another yet? When are you going to begin quarrelling? I love to listen in to you. You're as good as the radio."

"We don't quarrel any more," said Sue, and Robin nodded. They had both

made up their minds not to quarrel in front of big Jim, anyway!

As long as they were with their aunt or with Jim they were polite to one another. But when they were alone – oh, what a difference!

Auntie Ellen gave them fifty pence to spend. "Go to the shops and see what you can get," she said. So off they went. Jim didn't go with them, but he followed them soon after.

They saw a long stick of pink-coated peppermint rock in a shop. "Oooh, look! Peppermint rock in a great long stick!" said Sue. "It would take ages to suck. And look, it's got 'Margate' all down the middle. Even if we broke it in half, we'd still see 'Margate' written in pink in the middle."

"We'll buy a stick each," said Robin, and into the shop they went. But the stick was fifty pence. There were no twenty-five pence ones!

"Well – you could buy this fifty pence one, and break it into two equal halves," said the shopwoman.

So they bought the fifty pence rock,

and took it out of the shop. "I'll break it," said Sue.

"No," said Robin. "I will. You won't be fair." He caught hold of the stick and broke it himself. He held out one piece to Sue.

"Oh, you mean thing!" she said. "You've given me the smaller piece. You have!"

"I have not," said Robin. "*Mine's* the smaller if anything. *I* think they're exactly the same."

Sue snatched at Robin's and it fell to the ground. "You horrid girl – now you've made it dusty," said Robin. "You be careful I don't smack you. I've not only got the smaller piece of the two, I've got the dusty one. Horrid thing!"

A voice spoke behind them. "Aha! Two little squabblers again, I see. What's the

112

quarrel about *this* time?"

It was big Jim. Robin scowled at him. Sue turned away. "Go on, tell me," said Jim. "Maybe I can settle the matter for you."

"Well – we bought this fifty pence rock between us," said Sue, in a trembling voice. "And we thought we would have half each. But Robin gave me the smaller half, the mean thing."

"Let's see," said Jim, and he took the two pieces to measure against each other.

"Ah," he said. "I think this one is a bit longer than that one. I'll soon cure that!"

And he bit a piece of Robin's rock! He chewed it up joyfully. "Very nice. You'll enjoy it. Now let's measure it again."

He measured – but he had bitten such a big bit of Robin's that Sue's piece was now far too long. So Jim bit a piece of hers.

"Jim! Don't! It's *our* rock!" said Sue, almost in tears. She tried to snatch her piece from Jim, but he swung it out of the way.

"Now, don't snatch. You really are a horrid pair, aren't you – quarrelling and grumbling and snatching! Let me measure again!"

"You're a meanie, Jim," said Robin, in a rage, as Jim bit an enormous piece out of his rock. "There's hardly any of my rock left."

"Is that so?" said Jim, measuring again. "My word, you're right. Sue's bit is far too long now. Well, here goes!"

And off came another bit of Sue's. The two pieces or rock were now very small indeed, hardly a mouthful each. Robin and Sue glared at Jim.

"Give us what is left at once!" shouted

Robin. "Give our bits to us!"

"Now, now – don't be so impatient," said big Jim. "Aren't you going to give me any payment for deciding your quarrel for you? Look, these bits are exactly the same size now – aren't I clever! What will you give me for making them right for you?"

"Nothing!" shouted Robin, in a fine temper.

"Very well, then – I'll take my own payment for my trouble," said Jim – and do you know what he did? He popped both the last pieces into his mouth and began chewing them up.

Sue and Robin stared in despair. There was nothing to be done now. "We'll tell your mother," said Robin.

"She never listens to tell-tales," said Jim. "And she doesn't like squabblers, either. I wouldn't say anything if I were you. My word, that rock was good!" He turned and went away whistling. At the end of the road he called back to them, "It serves you right for quarrelling about something that didn't matter!"

Well, I suppose it did – but wasn't it a horrid, disappointing thing to happen!

You Simply
Never Know!

William had a lovely new kite. He was very proud of it indeed. It had a beautiful tail, and it looked as if it would fly very well indeed.

"I do so hope I don't lose it," said William to his mother, the first day he took it out to fly. "It's a big kite – and the wind's so strong it might break the string."

"Oh, I don't think so, dear," said Mother. "But, anyway, couldn't you just write your name and address on the kite? Then if it *does* fly off and somebody finds it, there's a chance they might be honest and bring it back."

William thought that was a very good idea. He scribbled his name and address on the kite as neatly as he could.

The kite certainly flew well. It leapt

up into the air at once, and tugged and pulled like a live thing. William shouted loudly.

"Here we go! Pull, kite, pull! That's right – go higher and higher! See if you can catch that cloud!"

The kite flew very high. It almost seemed as if it *was* trying to catch a cloud. William began to find it rather hard to hold the kite. It made him run a few steps!

"Hey, kite! Don't pull me so!" he cried. But the kite flew with the wind and dragged William along again. He came to the stream and fell in! To save himself he let go of the kite string – and away went the kite on its own in the windy sky. It chased the birds. It flew through a cloud. It even raced after an aeroplane.

When William picked himself up, soaked from head to foot, he was cross and upset. "Look at that! I've fallen into the stream, and I've lost my new kite. The very first time I flew it, too! Thank goodness I put my name and address on it. Perhaps it may be brought back."

Now the kite flew for miles and miles.

It flew over a great wood at last, and
then bumped into an enormous tree
– a tree that grew so high it touched
the clouds.

It was the Faraway Tree, of course,
that stood in the middle of the

119

Enchanted Wood. It banged against Moonface's door and lay still outside, tired out.

"Come in!" cried Moonface, thinking the bang was a knock. Nobody came in, of course, so Moonface opened the door. He was most astonished to see a kite there.

"What do *you* want?" he said, and picked it up. "What a beauty you are! Hallo – there's a name and address written here. 'William Wilson, Redroofs, Limming Village'. Do you

mean to say you've come all that way?"

The kite wagged its tail. Moonface called down the Faraway Tree. "Hey, Saucepan Man, are you there? Look what's come to see me!"

Saucepan looked, clanking as he came up to see. He was all hung around with kettles and saucepans.

"Have to take it back," he said, when he saw the name and address. "Come along. We'll go now. The boy it belongs to will be very upset if he thinks he has lost it."

The kite was too big to go down the Slippery-Slip that ran from the top of the Faraway Tree to the bottom, in the very middle of the great trunk. So Moonface walked out on to a broad branch with Saucepan, and threw the kite into the wind. It rose into the air at once, and Moonface and Saucepan hung on to the tail.

The kite took them gently down to the ground. Their weight was too much for it to fly away. Moonface picked up the kite and tucked it under his arm. It was really far too big to go there, and looked very peculiar. Saucepan carried the tail. The string ran on the ground like a long pale worm wriggling in and out.

Through the Enchanted Wood they went and over the ditch that surrounded it. Then they set off to catch the bus that went in the direction of Limming Village. The conductor said that the kite would have to go on top. It was an open-roofed bus so that was all right. Saucepan kept tripping over the tail as they went up the stairs, but at last they were safely sitting

on top of the bus, with the kite standing quietly beside them.

It was six o'clock before they arrived at Limming Village, and beginning to get dark. Moonface asked where Redroofs was, and then the two of them set off to take the kite to William.

They went to the back door, because they didn't think it was right to take kites to the front door. They knocked and William's mother opened the door.

She didn't see the kite at first. She only saw Moonface's shining round face and Saucepan all hung round with pans, wearing the usual saucepan for a hat.

"What a time to come selling kettles and saucepans!" she said, crossly. "No, I

don't want any."

"But look – we've brought back ..." began Moonface, tugging at the kite.

"So *you've* got something to sell, too," said William's mother. "I don't want anything at all. I don't buy at the door. Go away, please."

She shut the door. Moonface and Saucepan looked at one another.

"I suppose we do look a bit peculiar to her," said Moonface. "We forgot that. We'd better just scribble a message on the kite, leave it here, and go. After all, probably William's mother has never even heard of us."

So they scribbled a message on the kite, set it down near the kitchen door, gave a loud knock, and went down the path.

It was William who opened the door this time – and the first thing he saw was the kite!

"Mother! My kite – look! Somebody's brought it back!" he cried. "Who was it, do you suppose? Has anyone been to the door?"

"Dear me, yes – I wonder if *they* brought it back," said his mother. "Two most peculiar-looking people came – one with a round shining face, and one all hung about with pans and kettles."

"Mother!" said William. "Oh, Mother – could it have been – no, of course it couldn't." And then he saw the message scribbled on the kite.

Dear William,
Your kite fell in the Faraway Tree, so we brought it back. It's a beauty.
Yours with love
Moonface and Saucepan

"It was, it was!" shouted William. "Mother, which way did they go? Mother, I simply *MUST* find them. Don't you realise who they were – they're Moonface and Saucepan, from the Faraway Tree. Which way did they go?"

But his mother didn't know. William set off down the path, looking all about in the half-darkness. He heard a clanking noise some way down the road. That must be old Saucepan! He flew down the road after the noise.

The noise had gone round a corner. William rushed round at once. He could see something in the darkness not far off. *"SAUCEPAN!"* he yelled. *"MOONFACE!"*

The noise stopped. William rushed on eagerly.

"Wait for me, wait!" he cried, and at last he caught up with the noise, which had now begun again.

But what a dreadful disappointment! It was only Jim the farmer's boy going home on Cobber the horse, whose harness was jingle-jangling all the time.

It had sounded exactly like the noise old Saucepan's kettles and pans made.

I wish I could tell you that William found Moonface and Saucepan. But he didn't. They were gone, and he could have wept. What a chance, what a wonderful, marvellous chance – and he had missed it. Poor Mother – she would be disappointed, too, when she knew.

All the same, he was lucky, wasn't he? His kite had been brought safely back, he had had Moonface and Saucepan at his back door – and he's *still* got the little scribbled message on the kite. But oh, what a pity he *just* missed his two Faraway Tree visitors.

Teddy Bear
Is Naughty!

Alice was turning out her toy cupboard. Anything that was broken, or that she didn't want, she put into a heap. Mummy had said that she really must make room in the cupboard for her nice toys – they were just squeezed in every night, and they were getting spoilt.

"You have a lot of things in the cupboard that you don't want any more," said Mummy. "Clear them out."

So Alice was very busy. She found broken wheels off toy motor-cars. She found a broken signal. She found pages torn out of books, and loose feathers from her Indian head-dress. She found some old tubes of paint, too, half used.

She looked at them. 'I shan't want those any more,' she thought. 'I have a fine new paint-box now, that Uncle Ned gave me for my birthday. I'll throw those old tubes away, too.'

So they went on to the little pile of rubbish as well. Alice put them all into a cardboard box and set the box down by the waste-paper basket so that it could be taken away and put into the dustbin later on.

Now that night, when Alice was in bed, the toys woke up as usual and hopped out of the cupboard. The teddy bear saw the cardboard box and went over to look at it. He hoped that none of the toys he was friendly with had been put in there as rubbish.

They hadn't, of course. Teddy put his paw in and scooped over all the odds and ends. He saw the little tubes of colour, each one fitted with a tiny screw-on top.

Teddy unscrewed one of the tops. He sniffed inside the tube. It smelt funny.

'It's like a tiny tube of tooth-paste,' thought the bear. 'Perhaps it *is* tooth-paste – toy tooth-paste.'

He squeezed the tube a little, and, to his enormous surprise, out shot a long, coloured worm of red! The bear dropped

the tube hurriedly, and backed away.

He was very surprised. He didn't know that it was paint he had squeezed out. He really thought that a worm had popped out.

"You go back into your tube," he said to the red paint-worm. "Go on! Go back. I don't like you."

The red worm didn't go back. It lay on the floor, long and narrow and red, and it smelt funny.

It didn't move at all, so the bear soon didn't feel afraid any more. He poked the

131

worm a little and was surprised to find that his paw was red.

"Do any more worms live in the tubes?" he asked the red worm. But it didn't answer. The bear looked at the other tubes. There was one with a green label that looked nice and fat. Maybe a good long worm lived there. The bear longed to see if it did.

He lifted up the tube very cautiously and gave it a squeeze. Nothing happened at all. "Oh, I must take off your little front door," said the bear, and he unscrewed the tiny top. He squeezed the tube again.

At once an enormously long green worm shot out and curled round and round. The bear was half afraid again, but he couldn't help being excited.

'I've got a wonderful secret!' he thought to himself. 'I know where all kinds of exciting worms live. And I can make them come out of their holes. I'll tell the others – but I shan't tell the ragdoll, because he might think I oughtn't to do this. He says I meddle too much.'

The bear left the cardboard box and went over to the other toys. They were listening to the musical box, which the sailor doll had wound up. The ragdoll was over by the dolls' house, cleaning the windows. He was a good ragdoll, always doing some job or other.

"I say!" said the teddy bear, in a mysterious whisper. "I say! I know where worms live."

"Where?" said the clockwork mouse, in surprise.

"Aha!" said the bear. "That's my secret. I can make them come out of their holes, too. They are wonderful worms, all colours!"

"Don't be silly," said the small doll. "Worms are red. They're not any other colour. You're telling stories."

"I am *not*," said the bear crossly. "I tell you I do know where coloured worms live. And if you like to pay me something, each of you, I'll show you the worms and make them wriggle out of their homes."

The clockwork mouse longed to see the strange worms. He unwound the blue ribbon from his neck and gave it to the bear. "I'd like to see the worms," he said. "I haven't any money, but I'll pay you with this ribbon."

"Anyone else like to come?" said the bear. But nobody wanted to. So the bear took the little clockwork mouse across to the cardboard box and told him to watch.

Then he took up a tube of yellow paint and unscrewed the top. He gave the tube a sudden squeeze – and a long yellow worm shot out at once, almost on top of the mouse. He gave a squeal and ran away.

"What's the matter?" said the small doll, in surprise. "Did you really see a worm?"

"Oh, I did, I did," said the mouse, in a fright. "It was a yellow one – and it shot itself out at me and frightened me dreadfully."

Well, of course, after that, all the toys wanted to see the worms. The ragdoll was still cleaning the dolls' house windows, so he didn't come. But all the others did, after they had paid the teddy bear.

The small doll gave him the brooch off the front of her dress. The pink cat gave him one of her whiskers. The sailor doll gave him his hat. The big doll gave him a pair of her shoes. So the bear had quite a lot of things for himself. He put them carefully at the back of the toy cupboard.

Then he took the toys to the cardboard box. "There are three of the worms,"

he said, pointing to the red worm, the yellow one and the green one. "Now I'll show you where the blue worm lives, and make it come out and see you."

The toys watched in surprise. The bear unscrewed the top of the blue tube of paint, and gave it a big squeeze. A most enormous worm at once shot out, and almost touched the big doll's foot. She screamed.

"Oh, what a worm! The biggest I ever saw!"

"Make another, do make another!"

begged the sailor doll, excitedly. "Can you make a black one, a big, fat, black one? How clever you are!"

The bear felt pleased. He picked up the tube of black paint and took off the top. He squeezed it so hard that he emptied the tube completely of paint, and the worm that came out was so long and fat and black and wriggly that the toys gave squeals of fright and ran away.

The ragdoll looked up from his job of window cleaning in surprise. "What's the matter?" he said. "What are you afraid of?"

"Worms," said the clockwork mouse. The ragdoll looked astonished.

"There aren't any worms in this nursery," he said. "They live out-of-doors, not indoors."

"The bear's got plenty of worms over there," said the sailor doll. "He has really. He can make them. They suddenly jump out, red ones and yellow ones and all colours."

"This is most extraordinary," said the ragdoll and he went to see what the worms were. He stared at the squeezed-out tubes of paint, and looked very cross.

"You're a bad bear," he said to Teddy. "Do you know what you've done? You've used up all those tubes of paint! They're not worms. They're only paint."

"Oh," said the bear. "I thought they

were worms. They wriggle out like worms. It was fun making them."

"You've wasted all those tubes of paint," said the ragdoll, sternly. "And some child might have loved having them and using them. You are very, very bad. I am ashamed of you."

The bear began to feel miserable. He

140

knew he shouldn't have done it – but it was such fun. He stared at the coloured worms and wondered what to do. The ragdoll gave him a disgusted look and went back to his job.

The bear felt very unhappy. He felt that he really must do something about the paint-worms. He must put them back into their homes.

So the bear began to try and push all the worms back into the tubes. But, of course, he couldn't possibly, because

each worm went into a kind of horrid mess as soon as he pushed it. So he had to give it up and he went back into the toy cupboard looking most peculiar! He was red and yellow and blue and green and black in patches, for he had paint all over him! The toys looked at him in horror.

"Look at Teddy! He's like a patchwork quilt!" said the big doll. "Don't come near me, for goodness' sake, Teddy – you're in a dreadful mess!"

He certainly was – and when Alice found him the next day, how cross she was with him! "You've been messing about with my old paints!" she said. "Now I'll have to wash you and scrub you, and hang you out on the line to dry. You really are a very silly bear."

So he was washed and scrubbed in hot soapy water – and then, oh dear, he was pegged up on the line by both ears and he didn't like it at all.

The toys looked out of the window and saw him swinging dolefully on the line.

"Now see what happens to people who meddle with things that don't belong to them!" said the ragdoll. "They *always* get into trouble!"

He was right – but I feel sorry for the little bear.

He Didn't Know
What to Do

When James came home on prize-giving day, his mother had just come back from doing some shopping. His father was sawing wood in the back garden. James looked through the crack of the kitchen door and saw his mother putting away her groceries in the cupboard. He looked out into the garden and saw his father sawing busily.

You might think that, as it was prize-giving day, James would have rushed into the kitchen and then out into the garden to tell his mother and father all about it. But he didn't. He went upstairs into the dark little box-room, very quietly indeed, and shut himself in.

And there he stayed until it was suppertime, and his mother began to be very worried about him.

"Where's James?" she asked his father.

"I don't know," said the big man. "His bicycle is in the shed, so he must be home. But I haven't seen him. I was hoping he'd come and tell me all that had happened at the prize-giving. I know he won't have won a prize. James never does, and never will. But I should like to hear who had."

James's mother went upstairs and looked into the boy's bedroom. He wasn't there. She was puzzled, and called loudly.

"James! *JAMES!* Where are you? It's supper-time."

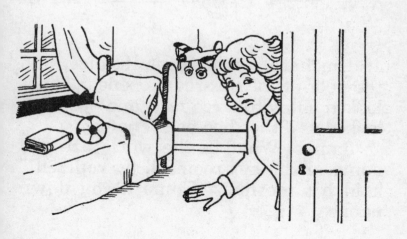

"I'm here," said a small voice, and the door of the box-room opened. James looked out with a red face, and eyes that looked as if they had been crying.

"James! What in the world are you doing in the box-room all by yourself!" said his mother. "Come along down at once."

So down went James, drooping his head as if he didn't want to look anyone in the face at all. His father looked up when he came in.

"Hallo, James! Did you bring home any prizes?"

"No, Dad," said James. "I was – I was bottom of my form. And you know, Dad, I've been trying really *hard* this term. I'll never be any good! I've got no brains at all. I can't even seem to remember my seven times table, and I've got right up to twelve times now."

"Sit down and eat your supper," said his father. "We'll have a talk about things."

"It's no good talking," said James. "Talking won't make brains come. I'm stupid and all the others laugh at me. I'm no good. I never will be. I haven't got any friends, and nobody asks me out to tea. They think I'm stupid. And I know you and Mother are ashamed of me, too!"

James burst into tears, and sobbed into his plate of cauliflower cheese.

"Now you listen to me, James," said his father, and he patted the boy's shoulder. "Why should we be ashamed of you, when you try so hard? If you didn't try, we *would* be ashamed. But we know that you've been away ill from school so much that you'll never catch up with the other boys, and we don't expect you to."

"But, Daddy, if only I was good at *some*thing," said poor James, wiping his eyes. "There's Tom now – he's not clever

either, but he can draw beautifully, and you should see how the other boys admire his pictures. And there's Peter – he can sing marvellously. And there's Jack – he can make model engines in a way I never, ever could. It's not fair. Even if the other boys aren't clever at lessons they've got some gift. And I haven't one at all. No wonder I haven't any friends. It's miserable."

"Well, if all this is making you miserable, we'll have to find some way out," said his mother. "Eat up your supper now and we'll all think hard."

James looked up after a while. "Well?" he said. "You've been thinking hard, and you haven't thought of a single thing I can do well, have you?"

"There *is* one thing you can do well," said his mother, suddenly. "You used to be very good at things like opening doors for people, carrying their parcels, giving up your seat in the bus, and so on, when you were smaller. Why not try and have the best manners in the whole school? I should be awfully proud of you then, because having good manners means being kind and courteous, patient and unselfish, all the things that really matter. If I thought our boy had the best manners in the school, that would mean more to me than you bringing home piles of prizes."

"Would it really, Mother?" said James, in astonishment. "But would it bring me friends? The other boys might laugh at me."

"Why not try it and see?" said his mother. "You have two weeks' holiday now. Practise a bit at home and on the neighbours, and then see what happens."

"All right, I will," said James. "I want to make you proud of me, I really do. I'll begin tomorrow."

But he began that very night, by opening the door for his mother to carry out the dishes, and then taking out the rest of the things himself!

The next day was quite exciting. James met old Mrs Brown, and he took his cap off at once. He didn't just tip it, but really raised it properly. And he stood and answered politely when Mrs Brown spoke to him. She beamed at him.

"Well, well, it's nice to see a boy being polite to an old woman like me. Mind you come along and see me next time I bake ginger biscuits. You'll know, because I'll put a card in my window with G.B. on, and then you can come knocking at my door."

"Thank you very much," said James. He walked on, and a boy from his school called to him: "Hey, James! Did I hear something about ginger biscuits?"

"You did," said James.

"Give me one when you get them," said the boy.

"Of course I will if I see you," said James, and the boy ran off.

"He's a decent fellow," thought the boy to himself. "It isn't many boys who would share ginger biscuits these days!"

James had to go shopping for his

mother that afternoon. He stood in the grocer's, waiting patiently to be served. The woman behind him sighed.

"Oh dear! I shall never get to the station in time to meet my friend."

"Well, you go in front of me and take my turn," said James at once, and he went behind the woman. She smiled at him gratefully.

"Well, it's a long time since I saw a boy so obliging. It's James Harrison, isn't it? My nephew goes to the same school as you do. He lives with me. You must come

to tea with him some time. I'm tired of always having rude boys brought home! You'll be a nice change!"

This was the first invitation to tea that James had had for months. He was very pleased.

When his turn came to be served, the grocer's wife put the things into his bag. Then she frowned and pointed to a parcel on the counter.

"Look at that! Old Mr White has left his goods, and we can't possibly deliver them to him. Silly old fellow!"

"I'll take them, if you like," said James. "I know where he lives."

"Thank you," said the grocer's wife, in surprise. "First time I've known a boy offer to do a thing like that! Look – here's a piece of chocolate cake for you."

"Oh, how lovely!" said James. He knew how nice the grocer's wife's cakes were, because her boy Peter sometimes used to bring slices to school for his lunch. Just at that moment Peter put his head round the door at the back of the shop. He made a face at James and laughed.

"Hallo, stupid!" he said. James went red. The grocer's wife looked round sharply at Peter.

"He's the only boy with good manners I've come across for a long time," she said to the grinning Peter. "If you were as good at manners as you are at singing, I'd be more than pleased. James, you come along tomorrow about suppertime and meet Peter's uncle. He's a merchant seaman and he'll tell you some marvellous stories."

"Oh, thank you," said James. He had often heard of Peter's wonderful uncle, and longed to meet him. He took his shopping bag, and old Mr White's parcel, and went out of the shop.

Mr White was in. He opened the door and exclaimed in delight at the parcel. "Well – to think someone's brought it for me, after all! That saves my old legs a long journey. Here's twenty pence for you, boy."

"No, thank you," said James. "The grocer's wife gave me a piece of chocolate cake. I was pleased to bring your parcel, sir. I didn't expect anything for it."

"Well, bless us all, here's a boy who really knows how to behave!" said Mr White. "I haven't met one for years. It's sad, but it's true. Young people haven't any manners, nowadays. They're rough and rude, selfish and greedy, and simply haven't time to be polite or kind. Well, I'm really pleased to meet you."

"Thank you," said James, going red and feeling rather uncomfortable.

"Wait a minute. I've got a book of

paper models of steamers and ships," said Mr White, and he hurried indoors. He brought back a big book. It looked most exciting. You cut out the ships, fitted them together, and made fine stand-up models. They had to have bits of flat wood stuck underneath, and then they sailed. It was really a marvellous book.

"Oh, great!" said James. "My – won't the other boys be thrilled! Thank you, Mr White."

He ran off with the book, and very soon met Jack, Mark and Freddie.

"Look what old Mr White gave me for taking his groceries to him!" he cried. "Model ships in a book all ready to be cut out! Would you like to do some? There are plenty for us all."

"That's decent of you," said Jack. "Another fellow might have kept the lot for himself. What about asking my mother to let you all come along after tea today and we'll do them together?"

"Great!" cried everyone, and ran home to tell their mothers. So after tea that day you might have seen four boys having a perfectly marvellous time cutting out model ships.

James went home first, carrying two ships. The others looked at one another.

"He's a good fellow," said Jack. "He may be bottom of the form and an awful dunce at lessons, but he's jolly nice, and he isn't a bit selfish."

"He's the best-mannered boy I've seen," said Jack's mother, pleased. "He even opened the door for me, and he carried that heavy washing upstairs. I wish *you* had a few ways like that, Jack. It would make people like you better. I'm tired of hearing mothers complain about your noisy behaviour. I'm sometimes quite ashamed of you."

That night James went to bed with a smiling face. His mother was right. Good manners and kindliness brought you smiles and gifts and friends much more quickly than anything else. He was really happy.

"I shall go on like this," he thought. "I enjoy it. It's nice to make people smile. I'll make Mother proud of me yet."

That was a year ago. Today, when James's mother met the headmaster of the school, she went red with pride at something he said.

"Mrs Harrison," he said, "I hope you'll never worry about James being low in form, because he more than makes up for it in other ways. He's the best-mannered, the kindest, and the most popular boy in the school! I shall be more sorry to lose James than any other boy!"

So James's mother was proud of him

after all; and if you happen to know him, you'll be lucky and will certainly want him for your friend. Wasn't it lucky that his mother thought of such a good idea?

Rufus
Pays Back

Jean and Donald were always busy in the garden. Their father had no gardener, and as he was working all day long, he never had much time for the garden, except in the late evening when he was tired.

So Jean and Donald did all they could to help. They were really very good little gardeners. I will tell you some of the things they did.

Well, every fortnight they sowed a long row of lettuce seed, not too thickly. Then, when the tiny green lettuces, came up, they thinned them carefully.

"If we don't thin them properly, the lettuces will be too close together when they are big, Jeanie," said Donald, "then they won't make nice hearts – and I do love eating the

heart of a lettuce, don't you?"

Then they hoed and weeded the garden well. Jean was very good at weeding. She knew how to use the hoe, too, and you should have seen her hoeing away at the tiny weeds showing their green heads above the earth!

"If I can hoe them up when they are small like this," she said to Donald, "they won't be any trouble at all! It's when weeds grow big and make seeds that fly all over the garden that they are really a nuisance."

Another thing they did was to stick the peas for Mother. As soon as the new-sown peas showed through the ground Donald fetched sticks, and the two children carefully set a double row of sticks down the peas, so that the tiny, curling tendrils could catch hold of the sticks and pull the pea-plants high into the air.

So you see they were very useful children, and their mother and father were proud of them.

One day, when Jean and Donald were busy hoeing and weeding, they heard a rich little song nearby. They looked up and saw a small robin redbreast, his large black eyes looking at them.

"Look! Look at that dear little robin," said Jean. "Oh, Donald – I do hope he gets tame. Don't let's frighten him at all."

The robin flew down almost to their feet, picked up a grub and flew back to

his perch. He swallowed the grub, cocked his head on one side, and sang a little song again, very short and sweet.

After that he followed the children about the garden whenever they appeared. He pecked up any worm or grub or caterpillar they dug up, and fed very well indeed. He became plump, and his red breast-feathers shone and glowed.

"We'll call him Rufus," said Donald. "That means red. He's so very, very red, isn't he!"

So they called him Rufus, and soon he was so tame that he would perch on the handle of their spade or fork, if they left it standing anywhere, or on the handle of their watering-can. He really was very sweet and the children loved him.

"I hope the next-door cat never gets him," said Jean anxiously. "She's such a clever cat at catching birds."

But Rufus was very sharp. As soon as he saw the big black cat jumping over the fence, he flew to the top of the lilac tree and warned all the other birds by making a curious ticking sound.

"Tick-tick-tick-tick," he said. "Tick-tick-tick-tick!"

Then all the birds would hear and be on the look-out. "He makes a noise like Daddy's fishing-rod line being unreeled!" said Donald. "Tick-tick-tick-tick-tick. Do you hear it?"

The children grew used to Rufus and his song and ticking noises. When they heard him singing they would whistle back cheerfully, and Jean would call out to him.

"Hallo, Rufus! Are you waiting for us? We're coming to garden now."

Then the little robin would fly down and wait about for the first grub.

Whenever they heard him "ticking"

the children would look round to see
what was the matter – and one day he
ticked and ticked! It was very, very hot,
and the children wore only their sun-
suits. They worked in the garden, and all
the time they heard the "tick-tick-tick"
of the robin.

They could see no cat in the garden,

and certainly there was no dog. What could be the matter?

Jean went in to tell Mother. "There's something the matter with Rufus," she said. "He keeps making that ticking noise. He's upset about something."

"I expect he feels hot, just as you do, and doesn't like it," said Mother. "Look – here is a shallow earthenware dish – take it out and fill it with water from the garden tap. Then put it down for Rufus to drink from and bathe in. After all, there is no stream near here, and no pond. I daresay he is very thirsty."

"Oh, I didn't think of that." said Jean, and she took the dish her mother gave her. She and Donald filled it under the garden tap, and then they put it down on the grass.

With a joyful, creamy song the robin flew down to it at once. He sipped water from it, tilting back his head, and letting it trickle down his throat.

"I always think it looks such a nice way to drink," said Donald, "just take a little water in your mouth, then hold your head back and let it run down your

170

throat. Oh, I say – what's Rufus going to do now?"

Rufus was paddling in the dish. The water was shallow, just up to the middle of his long legs. He suddenly put down his head, flicked out his wings, and scattered drops of water all over himself!

"He bathing! Oh, isn't he sweet?" said Donald. "Mother, come and look – Rufus has had a drink and now he is bathing!"

Rufus bathed about twenty times a day. Other birds came to bathe and drink too. Rufus chased them away if he was there. He seemed to know that Jean and Donald had really put out the bowl for him. "But you mustn't be selfish,

Rufus," said Jean, seriously. "You must let the others have a turn, too!"

The children went on with their gardening week after week. They sowed some lettuces. They watered the tomatoes in the greenhouse and watched one or two beginning to turn red. They watered the big marrow plants, and loved to see the marrows forming. Really, gardening was great fun.

But it had its tiresome times, too – and one of them was when the green caterpillars began to eat the new cabbages! Jean noticed one day that a good many of the cabbage leaves were full of holes. She went to see why – and then she called Donald.

"Donald! *Look* at our cabbages! Just look! There are big green caterpillars in almost every one!"

"Gracious!" said Donald. "How dreadful! Look at *this* cabbage – the heart is eaten almost away. Oh, Jeanie – we shall have to pick out all these horrid caterpillars and kill them."

It was a most unpleasant job. Jeanie hated it. She hated putting her hand into the heart-leaves of the big cabbages and trying to get hold of a soft, squirming caterpillar. She said it made her feel ill.

"I say! I wish Rufus would come and help!" said Donald at last. "Where is he?"

"Having a bath," said Jeanie, looking at the bowl on the lawn. "Oh – I know!"

Let's put his bowl here, in the middle of the cabbages! Then perhaps he will think to himself, 'Now why have they moved my bowl?' And he will guess we want his help with the caterpillars!"

So Donald carried the bowl to the cabbages, and set it down in the middle of them, where there was a little space. Rufus flew from bush to bush, following him in surprise. Why was Donald taking the bath away?

"Now listen, Rufus," said Donald, solemnly. "Here's your chance to pay us

174

back for making a pet of you! See these cabbages – and see this caterpillar I'm taking out of this one – well, we want your help with them, please!"

Rufus saw the fat green caterpillar, flew down to Donald's hand, and took it in his beak. He flew back to his bush, and in a second the caterpillar was gone!

"Did you see that?" said Donald, pleased. "Isn't he awfully tame now?"

The children went to work nearby, clipping the edges of the grass. They watched Rufus out of the corners of

175

their eyes. He flew down to his bowl to make quite sure it *was* his. He had a bath in it and flicked the water all over the cabbages. Then he sang a little song. Then he flew to a cabbage and sat on the top of it. His quick black eye caught sight of something moving in it, and he darted into the heart of the leaves at once. One quick peck and he was up again – with a giant green caterpillar in his beak.

"Oh, *good*!" said Jean, pleased. "He knows what we want him to do, Donald! Isn't he good? He's really paying us back for our kindness to him."

Rufus worked hard that morning. He visited every cabbage, stood on top of it, looked into the heart, and then if there was a caterpillar there he would find it and gobble it up.

"Mother, Rufus is a marvellous help to us," said Donald. "He's eaten about twenty caterpillars!"

Rufus was full up. He didn't seem to want any more to eat all that day, not even a wireworm that Donald offered him. He flew to a bough, and watched the children working. But next day he was hard at work on the cabbages again!

"He must have found about *thirty* caterpillars today!" said Jean. "He's getting fatter and fatter! Look how he sticks his little red chest out! Let's have a look at the cabbages, shall we? They won't be eaten nearly so much now."

They weren't. The new leaves that grew in the hearts of the cabbages were fresh and uneaten. The hearts were firm and solid. Rufus was proud of himself. Not one caterpillar would he leave in those cabbages.

Amanda
and the Bear

In the dolls' house there lived a small doll called Amanda. She was very neat and tidy, and she kept the dolls' house beautifully. The toys often saw her rushing about the house with brooms and dusters, and, dear me, how the front door knocker shone, and how white the steps were!

Amanda didn't only keep the dolls' house tidy. She kept the toy cupboard tidy, too. She swept out the corners, and she tidied up the bricks and the books. All the toys liked Amanda, except the teddy bear. He wasn't at all a tidy toy, and Amanda annoyed him.

"Let me tie your bow properly," she would say. "Dear, dear, you've sat down in some dust. Let me brush you! Oh, Teddy, please get up because I must sweep just where you are sitting."

All these things made the bear cross. He was a fat, lazy fellow, and he didn't see that it mattered whether his bow was crooked or not, and if he liked to sit down in the dust, why shouldn't he?

He began to be untidy on purpose to annoy Amanda. He undid his blue bow and let it hang loose, and he wouldn't tie it up. He got his paws very dirty, and wouldn't wash them, though Amanda actually put some water in a dolls' house bowl and brought it out to him with a clean towel.

He really was very naughty, because when Amanda tidied the bricks he shook the box and untidied them all again! And once when she had put the dominoes very neatly back in their long box, he emptied them all out, and pretended it was an accident!

"You really are a very untidy, clumsy bear," said Amanda patiently. She never got cross with anyone. She was a very hard-working little doll, always ready to do anything for anybody. "I suppose you can't help being clumsy or untidy, but dear me, you do make a lot of work!"

"I wish you wouldn't fuss round so," said the bear crossly. "You give me the fidgets! Whatever I'm doing you seem to find fault with – my bow wants tying, or my paws want washing, or something! I don't see what use you are, at all. You sweep up the dust – and more comes! You tidy the bricks – and next day someone plays with them and they're all untidy again. It's just a waste of time. You're a fusser."

"No, I'm not," said Amanda, quite hurt. "Someone has got to keep things

clean and neat and tidy."

The bear really did behave badly to Amanda. He spilt things. He upset everything he could. He pulled the carpet crooked. But Amanda always came hurrying to put everything right. Nothing would make her stop trying to keep things clean and tidy.

One night something peculiar happened to the bear. He was running across the nursery when he bumped into one of the toy soldiers. He knocked

him over and rolled right on top of him. The soldier's sword pricked him hard in the back.

"Oooh. You pricked me with your sword," said the bear.

"Well, you squashed me flat," said the soldier. "Sorry."

The bear got up. There was a little hole in his back where the soldier's sword had pricked him. Out of it came some specks of sawdust. The bear was filled with sawdust, you see.

Now the next day more sawdust came out of him. He didn't know it, and neither did the other toys. Only Amanda saw the sawdust on the floor when she came out of the dolls' house to tidy up the toy-cupboard.

"Look at that sawdust on the floor!" she said. "How untidy! I must sweep it up."

So she got her brush and dustpan and swept up all the sawdust she could find. She put it into the dustbin. Then she went to tidy the cupboard.

When she came out she was quite surprised to see more sawdust on the floor – quite a little line of it! The bear had taken a walk round the nursery, and wherever he had gone he had dribbled a little sawdust out of himself.

"How strange!" said Amanda, and fetched her dustpan and brush again. She swept it up, and put the sawdust in the dustbin.

She did this for two or three days, feeling very puzzled about it. Where in the world could so much sawdust be coming from?

On the fourth day the bear said he didn't feel very well. The toys looked at him.

"You look thin," said the toy rabbit.

"I *feel* thin," said the bear. "I feel all loose and thin and funny."

"You certainly look different!" said the sailor doll, anxiously. "You used to be so round and plump and solid. Now you are thin and baggy. What is happening to you?"

The bear looked sadly round. "I don't feel at all well," he said. "I've been feeling a bit peculiar ever since I rolled on top of one of the soldiers the other night, and his sword pricked me."

"Where did it prick you?" asked the

sailor doll. The bear turned round and showed him.

"Just there, in the middle of my back," he said. The sailor doll stared at the hole. As the bear moved, a few specks of sawdust came out.

"Oh, Teddy," said the sailor doll, with tears in his eyes, "a terrible thing has happened. There's a hole in you – and the sawdust inside has been coming out – which is why you are getting so dreadfully thin. Soon you will be nothing but skin."

The bear felt dreadful. "Can't you sew me up?" he asked.

"Yes – but you will never be your dear, fat, cheerful self again," said the clown. "If only we'd known, we could have sewn you up before you lost so much sawdust."

"What's the matter?" asked Amanda, coming up with a duster and broom.

"Oh, here's that awful tidy doll again," said the bear. "Go away, Amanda. I don't want my bow tied; I don't want my paws washed; I'm a poor ill bear who will never be any better."

Amanda was astonished. "What's the matter with him?" she asked.

"He got pricked on a soldier's sword, and he's lost half his sawdust inside," said the toy rabbit. "That's why he's gone so thin and miserable. We can sew him up but we can't make him fat again."

"Yes, we can!" said Amanda, beaming all over her funny little face.

"How?" said the clown, in surprise.

"Well, I've been noticing sawdust all over the carpet lately," said Amanda. "And you know what a tidy doll I am, always sweeping and dusting and clearing up. Well, whenever I saw the sawdust, I swept it up, and I put it in the dustbin. It's there still! The dustbin is almost full and I was wondering what I was going to do with it."

"What! You've really got my lost sawdust!" cried the bear.

"Yes, all of it," said Amanda happily. "So we can soon put you right, Teddy. I'll go and get it – and then we will stuff it back inside you and sew you up and you'll be perfectly all right in two minutes!"

Well, what an excitement there was then! The toy rabbit and the sailor doll ran to carry the dustbin. The curly-haired doll got a cup from the dolls' house and dipped it into the sawdust, and then emptied it into the hole in the bear's back. Amanda went to get her needle and cotton.

Soon all the sawdust was put back into the bear. "He's getting fat again," said the toy rabbit. "Press a bit more into his left leg, Clown. That's right. My word, he's looking himself

once more. That's good."

"We've put all the sawdust in," said the curly-haired doll. "Amanda, come and sew him up."

It didn't hurt very much. The bear was so pleased about everything that he didn't grumble at all when Amanda's tiny needle flashed in and out, sewing him up so neatly that you really couldn't see where the soldier's sword had pricked him.

"Thank you very much, Amanda," he said gratefully. "I've always been cross before because you were so tidy and fussy, but, dear me, how glad I am that you were, because if you hadn't been, you would never have swept up my sawdust, and I wouldn't have been my own fat jolly self ever any more. Thank you, Amanda. Just let me know if there is anything I can do for you at any time."

"All right," said Amanda. And after that she found plenty for Teddy to do! He moved the heavy things for her – the brick box and the domino box. He shook the mats in the dolls' house. He once swept the chimney and got himself all black, but didn't grumble at all when Amanda made him have a bath. She ties his bow every day – and he likes it!

"It did you good to lose your sawdust!"
says Amanda. And I really think it did!